I am a Penguin

First published in 2009 by New Holland Publishers (NZ) Ltd
Auckland • Sydney • London • Cape Town

www.newhollandpublishers.co.nz

218 Lake Road, Northcote, Auckland 0627, New Zealand
Unit 1, 66 Gibbes Street, Chatswood, NSW 2067, Australia
86–88 Edgware Road, London W2 2EA, United Kingdom
80 McKenzie Street, Cape Town 8001, South Africa

Publishing manager: Christine Thomson
Commissioned by Louise Armstrong
Editor: Georgina McWhirter
Design: Vasanti Unka
Front cover photograph: Adélie Penguin, Barbara Todd
Back cover photographs: King Penguin, Barbara Todd; author photo by
Steve Dawson

National Library of New Zealand Cataloguing-in-Publication Data

Todd, Barbara,1941-
I am a penguin / written by Barbara Todd; illustrated by Helen Taylor.
(I am a--)
ISBN 978-1-86966-242-6
1. Penguins—Juvenile literature. [1. Penguins.] I. Taylor, Helen J.
(Helen Joy), 1968- II. Title. III. Series.
598.47—dc 22

10 9 8 7 6 5 4 3 2

Colour reproduction by Pica Digital Pte Ltd, Singapore
Printed in China by SNP Leefung, on paper sourced from
sustainable forests.

PHOTOGRAPHY: Front cover/page 4: Adélie Penguin, Barbara Todd; page 6: Little Blue Penguin, BT; page 8: Rockhopper Penguin, JL Kendrick/
Department of Conservation Te Papa Atawhai, Crown Copyright; page 10: King Penguin, BT; page 11: King Penguin, BT; page 12: Adélie Penguin;
page 14: Yellow-eyed Penguin (left) and King Penguin (right), BT; page 15: Emperor Penguin (top) and Yellow-eyed Penguins (bottom), BT;
page 16: Emperor Penguin, BT; page 17: Emperor Penguins, Kim Westerskov; page 18: African Penguin, Nathalie Patenaude; page 20: Yellow-
eyed Penguin, BT; page 22: Rockhopper Penguins, Graeme Taylor/DoC (top) and JL Kendrick/DoC (bottom); page 23 (clockwise from top left):
Macaroni Penguin, BT; Royal Penguin, DoC; Snares Crested Penguin, Tim Higham/DoC; Fiordland Crested Penguin, Rosalind Cole/DoC; Erect-
crested Penguin, DoC; page 25: Little Blue Penguin, Rod Morris/DoC; page 26 (clockwise from top left): King Penguin, BT; Chinstrap Penguin,
JL Kendrick; White-Flippered Blue Penguin, Rod Morris/DoC; Gentoo Penguin, BT; Adélie Penguin, BT; page 28: Adélie Penguins, DoC; page 29:
Adélie Penguins, BT.

Also in this series:

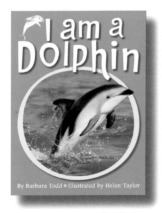

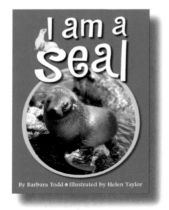

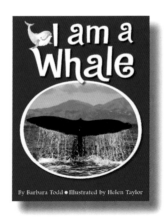

I am a Dolphin

ISBN 978 1 86966 264 6

I am a Seal

ISBN 978 1 86966 287 5

I am a Whale

ISBN 978 1 86966 298 1

I am a Penguin

By Barbara Todd • Illustrated by Helen Taylor

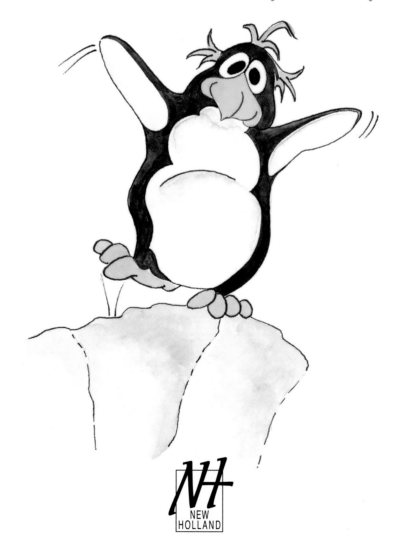

NH
NEW
HOLLAND

I'm a bird with two wings
But don't look in the sky
Because I am a penguin
And penguins can't fly!

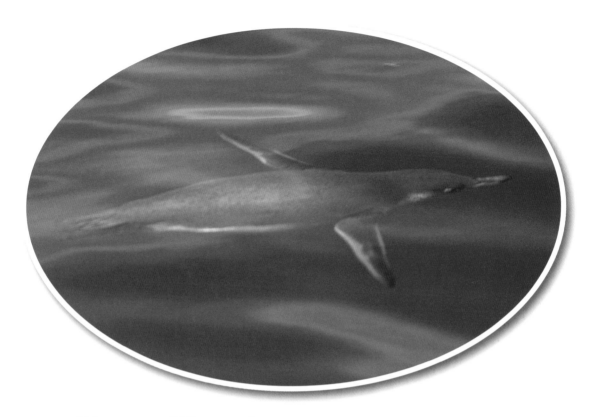

My flipper-like wings
Help me swim in the sea
Searching for food
That tastes good to me

I eat fish and squid
And tiny creatures called krill
I gobble all day
Till I've had my fill

BURP!

Once every year
When springtime is due
I lay eggs in a nest
There are usually two

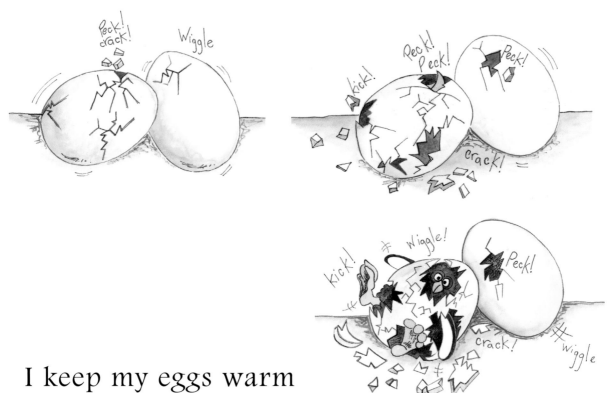

I keep my eggs warm
Till I see the first crack
Then I know that my chicks
Are ready to hatch

My new chicks are covered
With soft fluffy down
I feed them some fish
And they grow big and round

When they get older
New feathers grow in
Soon they are ready
For their first chilly swim

When my chicks leave the nest
I start to moult
My old feathers fall out
And I grow a new coat

Not every penguin
Looks exactly the same
Each type of penguin
Has its very own name

Some live where it's cold
Some live where it's hot
Some are quite big
And others are not

I'm an Emperor Penguin
The tallest of all
I live in a place
Where lots of snow falls

I have only one chick
And it needs lots of heat
It stays under my feathers
On the tops of my feet

I'm an African Penguin
I live where it's HOT!
The beaches are rocky
And the sun shines a lot

swelter

swelter

18

... I find cool shady places
To nest and to hide
So my two unhatched eggs
Don't become fried!

I'm a Yellow~eyed Penguin
I live where it's green
I nest under bushes
where it's hard to be seen ...

I talk to my friends
With long noisy calls
Some say that my voice
Is the loudest of all!

I'm a Rockhopper Penguin
My eyes are bright red
I have long yellow feathers
Sticking out from my head ...

Macaroni

Royal

I know lots of penguins
With yellow feathers too
Each type looks different
But they all look REAL COOL

Snares Crested

Erect-crested

Fiordland Crested

23

Do you think there's a penguin?
With feathers of blue?
Do you believe it?
Could it be true?

Yes, it is true
Though I'm not very tall
I'm a Little Blue Penguin
The smallest of all!

There are still lots of penguins
That you haven't met
Look very carefully
You can spot them, I bet!

I'm a
King ...

I'm a
Chinstrap ...

I'm a
White-flippered Blue ...

I'm an
Adélie ...

And I'm a
Gentoo ...

... We're all birds with two wings
But don't look in the sky
Because we are penguins
And penguins CAN'T FLY!

Did you know?

- Penguins have been around for a very long time – over 50 million years!

- There are 18 different types of penguin and they all live in southern parts of the world.

- Most penguins live for just 10 to 20 years, but Emperor Penguins can live up to 50 years.

- Long, long ago, there were GIANT penguins. The tallest penguin ever lived millions of years ago in New Zealand and was almost as tall as a grown man! Today, Emperor Penguins are the largest penguins and Little Blue Penguins are the smallest. Emperor Penguins are about as tall as an eight-year-old child and Little Blues are no bigger than a newborn baby.

- Emperor Penguins like to toboggan! They lie on their tummies and slide through snow to reach where they're going as quickly as possible.

- Little Blue Penguins live in New Zealand, where they are also known as Korora, and in Australia, where they are called Fairy Penguins. When Little Blue Penguins are born they are blind, almost naked, and are guarded by one of their parents for nearly three weeks. After eight weeks they are fat and covered in warm feathers and ready to leave the nest.

●Adélie, Gentoo and Chinstrap Penguins live in Antarctica and on snowy subantarctic islands. They are called the 'brush-tailed' penguins because they use their long tail feathers to sweep snow from their nests.

●The African Penguin, found only in and around Southern Africa, is also known as the Jackass Penguin. It gets this name from its noisy call that sounds like a donkey's bray.

●Yellow-eyed Penguins live only in New Zealand. Their Maori name is Hoiho, which means 'noise shouter'. These penguins are LOUD!

●Unlike most penguins, which lay two eggs each year, Emperor and King Penguins lay only one. Instead of keeping their egg in a nest, like other penguins, they keep it nestled on the tops of their feet under their warm fluffy tummy.

●Rockhopper Penguins are mini mountain-climbers. They hop up and down tall, rocky slopes, and often nest on top of steep cliffs.

Teacher/Parent Notes

Try these activities with your children for added learning and lots of fun!

Penguins live only in the southern hemisphere. Use a map or globe and work with children to identify the northern and southern hemispheres. Look in the southern hemisphere for places where penguins live. You can start with Antarctica, the coldest place on earth and the home of Emperor Penguins. Move to the Antarctic Peninsula, one home of the 'brush-tailed' penguins (see page 31), and then on to subantarctic islands around the globe. Head to Australia's Macquarie Island, the only place in the world where Royal Penguins breed. Don't forget New Zealand and its subantarctic islands, which are home to seven different species of penguin. Finally, move to the hotter climate of the banded penguins. They live on the Galapagos Islands, in Africa and in South America.

Ask children to pick one type of penguin and make a suitable nest for that penguin to lay its eggs in. Think about that penguin's habitat. The 'brush-tailed' penguins live where it is cold and snowy. They use stones, pebbles and whatever other material they can find to build their nests. In slightly warmer climates penguins make use of grass, twigs and feathers, while penguins in hot climes often dig burrows in the ground. Emperor and King Penguins, on the other hand, don't make a nest at all! (See page 31.)

In the cold Antarctic winter, Emperor Penguins huddle together to stay warm and protect their eggs. Turn on a cold fan and ask your children to huddle together with the fan blowing on the group. Now get the children on the outside of the circle to swap with those in the centre. Ask them when they felt coldest – when they were in the middle of the huddle or on the outer edge? Those in the middle should have been much warmer as the centre is less exposed to the wind. Explain to the group that Emperor Penguins huddle together much like this, taking turns changing position so that no penguin gets too cold.

Use an encyclopedia or the Internet to look up places where penguins live. What other animals live in the same location? Learn more about that country's penguins and the other inhabitants of these places. Yellow-eyed Penguins are found only in New Zealand and there are not very many of them. Why is that?

Emperor Penguins protect their eggs from the cold by keeping them under their warm feather-covered bellies. Get two raw eggs and carefully wrap one in cotton wool or padded material. Leave the other egg unpadded. Place both eggs in the freezer, shut the door and leave them for 15 minutes. Take the eggs out and break them open into separate glass bowls. Do you see a difference? Tip: So as not to let the eggs go to waste, use them in cooking or baking after your experiment is complete.